The Doors' Fire

Dyva Gibbs

The Door's Fire

Dyva Gibbs

Art Cover by The Little French eBooks

Published by The Little French eBooks

© The Little French's Media 2024

License Notes

This eBook is licensed for your enjoyment only. This eBook may not be resold or given away to other people. If you would like to share this book with another person, please purchase an additional copy for each person you share it with. If you're reading this book and did not purchase it, or it was not purchased for your use only, then please return to smashwords.com and purchase your copy. Thank you for respecting the hard work of this.

A dimly lit L.A. rehearsal space, 1965.

The air crackled with a mix of cigarette smoke and creative tension. Jim Morrison, clad in leather pants and an open silk shirt, paced the room, his eyes gleaming with manic energy. Ray Manzarek hunched over the keyboard, noodling out a bluesy riff, while Robby Krieger strummed his guitar in counterpoint. John Densmore sat poised behind the drum kit, keeping the beat.

Jim swayed to the music with eyes closed. "Yeah, Ray, keep it loose, like snakes in the desert sun... Robby, let your strings wail like a coyote at the moon. John, that steady pulse, man, the heartbeat of the universe."

Ray looked up, a smile on his face. "You feeling it tonight, Jim? Got a song brewing in that cauldron of yours?"

Snapping his eyes open, Jim gave a mischievous grin. "Not just for me, Ray. It's time we stopped playing other people's tunes and unleashed the beast within each of us. We've got stories burning inside, poems screaming to be sung."

Strumming a thoughtful chord, Robby said. "I don't know, Jim. Writing our own stuff... that's a different beast altogether."

"Yeah, man. It's one thing to play covers and get the crowd riled up. But putting our own words out there, that's putting ourselves on the line," John said.

Jim, stepping closer and his voice dropping to a conspiratorial whisper, said. "Precisely! That's the whole damn point. We're not just musicians, we're poets of the night, prophets of the electric storm. We need to paint our own landscapes, ignite the fire with our own truths, even if they scorch the earth."

Ray's eyes gleamed. "I like the fire metaphor, Jim. But where do we start? How do we tap into this... wellspring you're talking about?"

A sly smile played on Jim's lips. "Look inside, brothers. Look at the shadows dancing on the walls, the whispers in the alleyway, the dreams that haunt you in the dead of night. Let them bleed onto the canvas of sound. We'll riff, we'll jam, we'll howl at the moon until the melody takes shape."

Robby gave a hesitant smile. "You make it sound so easy, Jim."

Dramatically flinging his arms wide, Jim said. "Because it is, Robby! We are the catalysts, the conduits. The music is already there, waiting to be born. We just have to tear down the walls of convention and let it roar."

John tapped his drumsticks on the rim. "Alright, alright, Jim, you've got me itching to unleash the thunder. Let's see if we can conjure some lightning, shall we?"

Ray said with a twinkle in his eye. "Hit it, brothers! Let's paint the night with our own colors."

The room exploded into a cacophony, a raw and primal expression of their collective energy. Jim's voice, a wild incantation, rose above the din, weaving stories of rebellion and self-discovery. Music became a living entity, morphing and evolving under their hands, a testament to their newfound creative freedom.

As the final notes faded, a hush fell over the room. The bandmates exchanged glances, a shared grin spreading across their faces.

***

B_{eer} bottles littered the table, smoke hung heavy in the air. The Doors slumped in chairs, a tense silence between them.

Slouching with his signature brooding, a bottle dangling precariously from his fingers, Jim said. "So, gentlemen. Another night, another crowd hypnotized by our borrowed plumage. How many covers shall we do before we shed this skin and become ourselves?"

Ray stroked his chin and tried to calm down the singer. "Easy, Jim. We built our name on these classics. People love them. And hey, playing blues standards ain't exactly servitude."

Jim gave a sardonic flicker of a smile. "But it's not liberation, Ray. We're playing someone else's revolution, someone else's blues. We have our own stories to scream, our own demons to dance with."

Robby picked up a guitar and strummed a wistful melody. "I've got some chords, Jim. A whisper of something, waiting to be fleshed out."

Jim's eyes lit up. "That's the spark, brother! Let's fan it into a flame. Forget the roadmaps, the well-worn paths. We're explorers, Ray, cartographers of the soul. Let's chart our own territories, paint our own landscapes with sound."

John was ever the pragmatic one. "But where do we even start? Songwriting ain't exactly our strong suit."

Jim leaned forward. "It's inside us, John, in the echoes of our own hearts. Remember those late-night jams, the riffs that spun themselves from the ether? We had something back then, a raw, unfiltered energy. Let's tap into that chaos, give it form and voice.

"Chaos, eh?" Ray demanded. "That's your middle name, Jim. But I ain't opposed to a little creative anarchy. Besides, you spin words like silk, brother. We feed you the music, you weave it into poetry. A partnership forged in fire."

Jim raised his bottle to toast. "To fire, then! To liberation, to exploration, to exorcising our own inner demons onto the sonic canvas. Who's ready to become architects of their own reality??

***

The California sun beat down on the dusty L.A. street, shimmering off the chrome of parked cars and casting long shadows from the palm trees. Robby Krieger, guitarist for The Doors, squinted through the glare, his fingers drumming a restless rhythm on the worn leather of a diner booth. Inside, the jukebox crackled and spat out the incendiary blues of "Hey Joe," Jimi Hendrix's guitar weaving a tale of murder and escape.

Robby's head bobbed, his ear catching the melody's simplicity, its raw power. It was a bare-bones structure, a blues riff built on repetition and tension, and yet, it captivated him. He could almost feel the heat of the desert highway, the taste of dust on his tongue, and the adrenaline rush of a desperate journey.

The song ended, replaced by the raucous swagger of "Play with Fire" by the Stones. Jagger's voice, a sandpaper growl, dared the listener to ignite the flames of desire, to burn bright and reckless. Robby's fingers tapped out a counterpoint on the table, a bluesy riff echoing the Stones' rhythm but with a different edge. His mind raced, melodies swirling like smoke in the air.

He closed his eyes, picturing Jim Morrison, the band's enigmatic frontman, lost in the lyrics he'd been sculpting for weeks. Jim's words whispered of darkness and dreams, of journeys into the unknown. Robby needed a sound to match, a sonic canvas for those wild visions.

Suddenly, a chord struck him – a minor seventh, sharp and dissonant, hanging in the air like a question mark. He followed it with a descending blues lick, the echo of "Hey Joe" woven into the fabric of the new phrase.

He snapped his eyes open, a spark of excitement igniting in their depths. This was it. This was the seed of something new, something dangerous and intoxicating. A song that would burn with the heat of the desert sun, dance with the shadows of the night, and roar with the defiance of a generation hungry for something real.

Robby grabbed his guitar, his fingers flying across the strings, fleshing out the nascent melody. The diner faded away, the clatter of plates and chatter of customers replaced by the throb of his amplifier, the growl of his distortion pedal. He was lost in the music, channeling the fire of "Hey Joe," the swagger of "Play with Fire," and the raw energy of The

Doors into a song that would become their anthem.

The sun dipped below the horizon, painting the sky in fiery hues. Robby, face flushed and hair damp with sweat, emerged from the music, a grin splitting his face. He had found his spark, and The Doors, he knew, were about to ignite the world.

***

The air crackled with anticipation in the Doors' rehearsal space. Robby Krieger, his guitar slung low, shuffled in, a hesitant smile playing on his lips. He cradled a half-formed melody, a whisper of words clinging to it like fireflies to a moonlit night.

"Alright, fellas, gather 'round," he said, strumming a lazy chord. "Got something new I been workin' on."

John Densmore, the band's heartbeat behind the drums, leaned forward, eyes gleaming. Ray Manzarek, the alchemist of keys, tapped a rhythmic pulse on his organ. Jim Morrison, the enigmatic frontman, stood in the shadows, a flicker of intrigue dancing in his eyes.

Robby's fingers danced across the strings, weaving a melody that was both familiar and strange. The lyrics, raw and vulnerable, spoke of heartbreak and longing, of shadows dancing on the edge of dawn.

"This is good, Robby," Ray said, his voice a low rumble. "But it needs...something."

John, ever the percussionist of ideas, snapped his fingers. "Latin beat," he declared. "Give it some spice, some swagger!"

Robby's brow furrowed, and then a smile broke through. He began to tinker, the melody morphing under his touch, a syncopated rhythm snaking its way through the chords. The Doors, a single organism, responded in kind. John's drums became a rolling thunder, Ray's keys a smoky whisper weaving through the rhythm. Jim, his voice a low growl, began to fill the spaces with words, painting pictures with metaphors, leaving just enough darkness for the listener to explore.

"Moonlight drippin' from the sky, shadows whisperin' lies," he crooned, each syllable a brushstroke on the canvas of sound. "Hearts beatin' like a drum, lost in the city's hum."

The intro, once a simple strum, became a sonic explosion under Ray's touch. His organ, a hungry beast, roared to life, its notes cascading like molten lava. The Doors, no longer a band, were a force of nature, channeling the raw energy of the night into a single, electrifying moment.

By the time the last note faded, the room was silent, the air thick with the aftershocks of creation. Robby, his face flushed with adrenaline, looked at his bandmates, a question hanging in the air.

"What do you think?" He asked.

John grinned, a wolfish gleam in his eyes. "We just wrote a masterpiece, Robby."

Ray nodded, his fingers still dancing on the keys. "This is gonna take the world by storm."

Jim, his eyes closed, a faint smile playing on his lips, simply said, "Light my fire."

And in that moment, amidst the echoes of drums and organ, a legend was born. They have crossed a threshold, stepped into the unknown, and emerged with a newfound fire in their eyes. The Doors had found their anthem, a song that would forever echo through the canyons of time, a testament to the transformative power of collaboration, the magic that happens when inspiration meets refinement, and the raw, untamed spirit of a band on the precipice of greatness.

The Doors have opened, and their own music, born from the depths of their souls, would forever echo through the halls of rock and roll history.

Milton Keynes UK
Ingram Content Group UK Ltd.
UKHW050429280324
440101UK00016B/1003